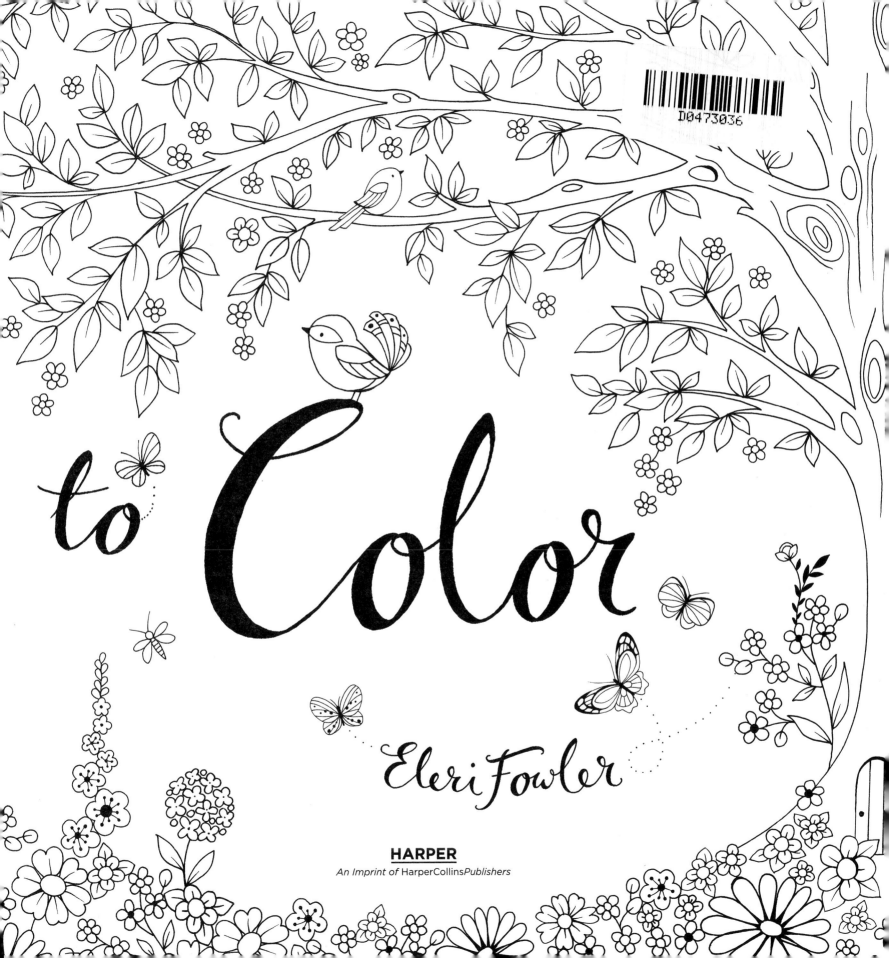

to Color

Eleri Fowler

HARPER

An Imprint of HarperCollinsPublishers

For my wonderful parents,
Keith and Gwenda.
In loving memory of Iris,
a truly beautiful flower.
–E.F.

Joyous Blooms to Color
By Eleri Fowler
Copyright © 2016 by HarperCollins Publishers
All rights reserved. Printed in the United States of America.
No part of this book may be used or reproduced in any manner whatsoever without written
permission except in the case of brief quotations embodied in critical articles and reviews.
For information address HarperCollins Children's Books,
a division of HarperCollins Publishers, 195 Broadway, New York, NY 10007.
www.harpercollinschildrens.com

ISBN 978-0-06-244380-9

The artist used a pencil, paper, fineliner pen, and computer to create the illustrations for this book.
Typography by Whitney Manger
16 17 18 19   PC   10 9 8 7 6 5 4
❖
First Edition

This book belongs to

_____

Welcome to my garden!
This book is a window into my sketchbook:
full of all the wonderful landscapes I've enjoyed both
here in Wales, where I live, and also a glimpse at the more
exotic flora that I've discovered during my travels around the world. I
have included a selection of illustrations of my favorite flowers and garden
scenes, and dreamed up a few of my own. Now, you can make these designs
your own! The choice is yours—experiment with colored pencils, gel pens, or
felt-tip pens. Do try a few test doodles to make sure your pens don't bleed through
the paper! If you are using colored pencils, try building up different shades and tones
of color within your design. This will add depth and mimic the variety of different
colors that exist in nature. The best way I've found to mix two or more colors together
is to layer each color in turn from lightest to darkest. That way, you can control the
intensity of the color. If you're feeling a bit daring, try using watercolors! (But be
sure to let them dry before turning the page.) Once you've filled your pages with
glorious color, why stop there? You can be sure I won't be limited to just
coloring—my copy of the book will be bursting with little embellishments
like gems, sequins, and glitter. Be creative! I love that no two finished
books will look alike: embrace that! The most important thing
is to experiment and have fun.

Eleri

My Influences

Nature has a massive influence on my work. I love to go on long walks in the country and along the coast. My area of Wales is bursting with beautiful gardens and rolling hills, which means inspiration is just outside my front door!

My biggest source of inspiration, however, is travel. It is my absolute passion. I have spent quite a lot of time in Southeast Asia, which is my love, and where I thrive. The abundance of nature, the animals, and breathtaking scenery cannot fail to fill your imagination. I feel so lucky to have a job that lets me work as I travel about, so I always make sure that I have a sketchbook and laptop on hand to start the next project wherever inspiration strikes. Coming home from a trip, I always feel extra energized and full of creativity!

Behind the Scenes:
How I Create My Art to Color

I always start a project with a simple sketch using a mechanical pencil. I am a bit of a perfectionist, so one of my favorite tools in the world is my 0.35mm pencil, as it gives such a smooth, precise line. I like to work on layout paper as it is semitransparent, which is great for tracing. Perhaps I'm a bit old-fashioned, but I like to stick to traditional drawing methods as much as possible and only use the computer for final tweaks for print.

To create my illustrations, first I'll sketch out a rough shape—laying out the main elements in the piece. Then I'll trace over it, adding in more details. I'll repeat this stage a few times until I end up with a piece that I am happy with. Then, I redraw the final image using a black fineliner pen (0.05 is my preference as, just like with my pencil, it gives a very thin and accurate line).

TO unpathed WATERS, undreamed SHORES

SHAKESPEARE

All good things are wild and free

THOREAU

A THING of beauty IS A Joy for ever

KEATS

Earth
IN FLO

Earth laughs in flowers. —EMERSON

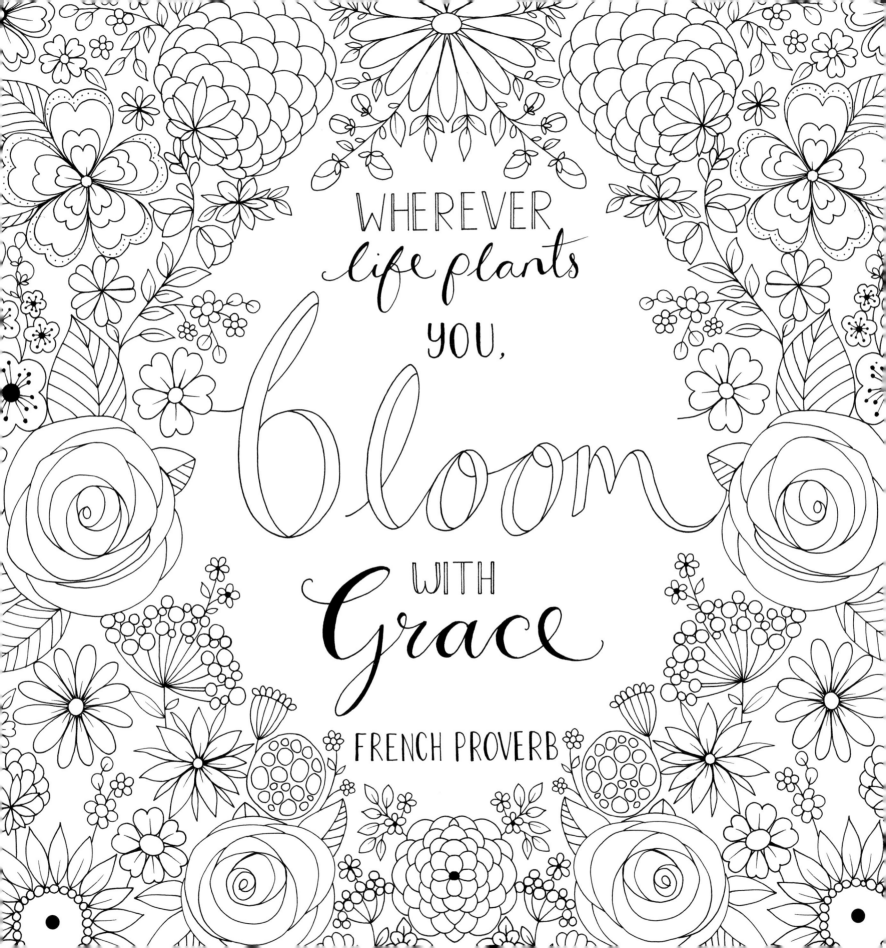

WHEREVER *life plants* YOU, *bloom* WITH *Grace*

FRENCH PROVERB

I Believe a LEAF of grass IS NO LESS than the Journey work OF THE STARS

WHITMAN

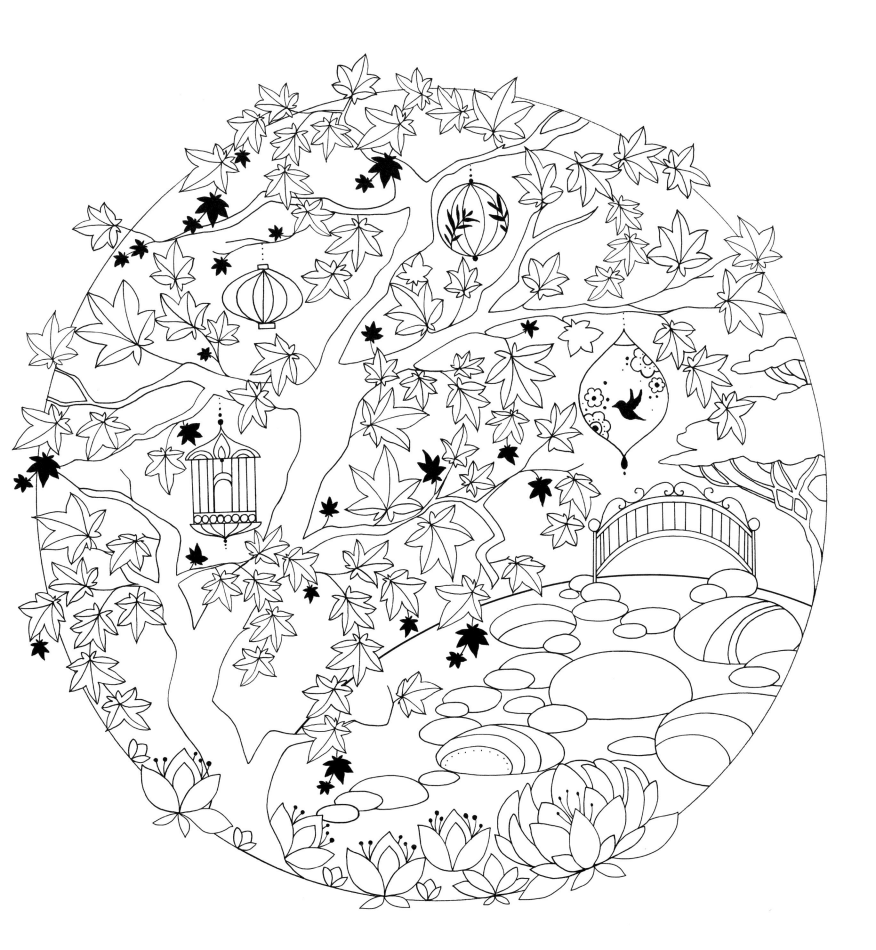

I AM THE Lover of Uncontained AND IMMORTAL Beauty

— EMERSON —

while we are thoroughly ALIVE

ELIOT

About the Author

I have always loved all things creative, and can't imagine myself doing anything else but art. I studied illustration at university, but since working as a full-time artist, I've found myself experimenting with embroidery and paper cutting, which gives my art depth and texture. After graduating, I worked as an in-house illustrator for a greeting card company, and now I work for myself and have my own card collections.

I love working with patterns, as they really let me think technically. I also really enjoy the simplicity of the continuous line, so the opportunity to fill up this book with oodles of gorgeous patterns was an exciting one for me. I really hope you love coloring it as much as I loved drawing it!

www.elerifowler.com

List of Quotes

"Earth laughs in flowers."—Ralph Waldo Emerson

"I am the lover of uncontained and immortal beauty."—Ralph Waldo Emerson

"Live in the sunshine, swim the sea, drink the wild air."—Ralph Waldo Emerson

"I will not follow where the path may lead, but I will go where there is no path, and I will leave a trail."—Muriel Strode

"Bring me the sunset in a cup."—Emily Dickinson

"I went to the woods because I wished to live deliberately."—Henry David Thoreau

"All good things are wild and free."—Henry David Thoreau

"Wherever life plants you, bloom with grace."—French proverb

"To unpathed waters, undreamed shores."—William Shakespeare

"Seek happy nights to happy days."—William Shakespeare

"Every leaf speaks bliss to me."—Emily Brontë

"I believe a leaf of grass is no less than the journey work of the stars."
—Walt Whitman

"A thing of beauty is a joy for ever."—John Keats

"Those who wish to sing always find a song."—Swedish proverb

"We can never give up longing and wishing while we are thoroughly alive."
—George Eliot